ADIEU
PERFECTIONS
A Satire

CHARLES MWEWA

To the permanent betterment of race relations
across the globe

CONTENTS

A great deal has been done and progress has been made in race relations. However, remnants of historical injustices, usually unintended, do show up in standards applied to groups that have, historically, been marginalized. For example, they may be required to go far and beyond their ability to show that they can do a job or run a government or corporate department. The same standards may not be set or applied to the dominant group. Indeed, a lot can still be done. For the good that is being done, we should applaud those, and laugh at the past. This little book is a satire.

Las Vegas, Nevada, USA
August 2023

A SATIRE

Oh, we have come a long way
And sometimes, it seems not to
sway
When the only perfect, the only
sound
Would be judged on no other
ground
But on being White and Western
While all others would follow this
pattern;
We are relegated to the secondary
class
And disparaged as being but only
crass.

*PERFECTION
IS A MYTH*

Let us start the song, Oh, Mother
And let me shake your grave up,
Father,
For the times are here now with us
And all should not and presently
pass
Whether it be women or the
disabled
Whether it be men of color or the
abled
Whether they be unilingual or native
And whether they be activists or
passive.

*THE
MINORITIES
ARE'NT
PERFECT, SO
IS THE
MAJORITY*

They were dragged out of the malls
Others were lynched on stoned
walls
When they wanted to rise and speak,
They were blamed for not reaching
their peak;
They were publicly shamed for their
color
And paraded as merchandise at the
parlor
For they were judged unworthily
imperfect,
Because they'd not measure up to be
perfect.

SOMETIMES OUR
IMPERFECTIONS,
MAY BE OUR
ASSETS

Like animals to be tamed, they were
branded
Like fowls to be slaughtered, they
were banded
Their humanity was trodden at the
pride altar
Their native names, they did change
and alter.
They were made to forget who they
were
Not to return home or be
remembered there;
They lost all connections to
ancestral land,
They only fed at crumbs of the
master's hand.

*NATIVE
TRAITS ARE
JUST AS FINE*

They sang melodies out of the wild
They sent their kids to mines unmild
If they survived, they cooked
porridge
If they deserted, they hunted for
partridge
Shout, O, little wondering bird, sing
a solo
So that the perfector can win the
polo
But do not overdo it, for then and
as now
The unroyally born, receive now
wow.

*ACCEPTANCE
SHOULD NOT
REQUIRE
OVERDOING*

The dirge never got to get its true
meaning
Even in death, their story was
demeaning
And where they were buried, its
unknown
Only the song of a parrot became
known
Oh, Sister, O Brother, we have
come here
After many centuries of gloominess
there
So, even their royal names are not
known
Never would they ever dream to be
renown.

*CREATIVITY
IS NOT A
MONOPOLY
OF THE
DOMINANT
SOCIAL
GROUP*

Shame be on those who carried the
whip
Which they fastened to have bitter
grip
To break a Black woman's beautiful
buttock
Which they desired to plump out of
stock.
Black backs that were meant for
flattery,
Became subjected to perpetual
battery;
They toiled unendingly, lands to
make green
But their own dignity, was lowered
as unclean.

*HISTORICAL
IGNORANCE
MUST NOT
JUSTIFY
RACIAL
BATTERY*

The leaders of men and those who
ruled;
The disabled they upbraided and
booed.
Jobs they denied them, forbidden to
earn
How they were born, became their
chain.
They were forced to beg, not to
work;
Their defect was used as badge and
fork.
They did not let them have any
access,
For buildings which they built had
staircases.

*THE
DISABLED
ARE ALSO
ABLE*

They had zero chance to own
property
All they longed for was claimed
champerty
They were regarded as volid social
misfits
For all good things, they deemed
them unfit
Come, Modern Man, hear this
lamentation,
Sick or well, they were insulted on
plantations.
They spent unbilled time in the
sun's heat;
For water, they received nothing but
cold feet.

*PROPERTY
OWNERSHIP
SHOULD NOT
DEPEND ON
RACIAL
PREJUDICE*

They invaded *their* native lands and
wealth
And left *them* poor and in very bad
health.
Then they came and displaced the
Aboriginals
And they claimed that they were the
originals.
Their way of life, they completely
reneged.
Where *they* hunted, they placed very
big rigs.
Their children, they condemned to
residentials.
And many died, refused of their true
credentials.

*STOLEN
LANDS
MUST BE
RECLAIMED*

Rights, what rights would a woman
have?
She never got to appreciate the
word love.
An object of men's lust, a
commodity she was.
Her own husband demanded she
called him boss
At home, she worked without any
compensation;
When he died, she received no
honor or pension.
Oh, woman, equality you were
denied for no reason,
And until recently, you were not
even a person.

*WOMENAND
BLACKS
HAVE ALWAYS
BEEN
HUMAN*

When a White boss says to a Black
employee,
"Thou shouldst be above board,
mind thee,"
He might surreptitiously be
demanding perfection.
And when a Black boss say to a
White worker,
"Your performance is not subject to
inspection,"
He may be claiming that she may
have to work harder.
And what are we acknowledging in
territorial recognitions?
Nothing except that it's not in *Indian
Act* provisions.

*RACE
HISTORY CAN
BE VERY
DELETERIOUS*

ABOUT THE AUTHOR

Charles Mwewa (LLB; BA Law; BA Ed; LLM) is a prolific author and researcher, poet, novelist, lawyer, law professor and Christian apologist. Mwewa has written no less than 40 books and counting in every genre and has exhibited his works at prestigious expos like the Ottawa International Book Expo and is the winner of the Coppa Awards for his signature publication, *Zambia: Struggles of My People*.

SELECTED BOOKS BY THIS AUTHOR

1. *ZAMBIA: Struggles of My People (First and Second Editions)*
2. *10 FINANCIAL & WEALTH ATTITUDES TO AVOID*
3. *10 STRATEGIES TO DEFEAT STRESS AND DEPRESSION: Creating an Internal Safeguard against Stress and Depression*
4. *100+ REASONS TO READ BOOKS*
5. *A CASE FOR AFRICA?S LIBERTY: The Synergistic Transformation of Africa and the West into First-World Partnerships*
6. *A PANDEMIC POETRY, COVID-19*
7. *ALLERGIC TO CORRUPTION: The Legacy of President Michael Sata of Zambia*
8. *BOOK ABOUT SOMETHING: On Ultimate Purpose*
9. *CAMPAIGN FOR AFRICA: A Provocative Crusade for the Economic and Humanitarian Decolonization of Africa*
10. *CHAMPIONS: Application of Common Sense and Biblical Motifs to Succeed in Both Worlds*
11. *CORONAVIRUS PRAYERS*
12. *HH IS THE RIGHT MAN FOR ZAMBIA: And Other Acclaimed Articles on Zambia and Africa*
13. *I BOW: 3500 Prayer Lines of Inspiration & Intercession from the Heart: Volume One*
14. *INTERUNIVERSALISM IN A NUTSHELL: For Iranian Refugee Claimants*
15. *LAW & GRACE: An Expository Study in the Rudiments of Sin and Truth*
16. *LAWS OF INFLUENCE: 7even Lessons in Transformational Leadership*

INDEX